SHOW AND TELL

Why should you be kind to others?

Katiuscia Giusti

www.av2books.com

Go to **www.av2books.com,** and enter this book's unique code.

BOOK CODE

K274232

AV² by Weigl brings you media enhanced books that support active learning.

First Published by

aurora
www.auroraproduction.com

Aurora Production AG
Tellsgasse 19   CH-6460 Altdorf UR 1
Switzerland

Published by AV² by Weigl
350 5th Avenue, 59th Floor New York, NY 10118
Websites: www.av2books.com   www.weigl.com

Library of Congress Control Number: 2014941333

ISBN 978-1-4896-2287-7 (hardcover)
ISBN 978-1-4896-2288-4 (single user eBook)
ISBN 978-1-4896-2289-1 (multi-user eBook)

Printed in the United States in North Mankato, Minnesota
1 2 3 4 5 6 7 8 9 0   18 17 16 15 14

052014
WEP090514

MORAL OF THE STORY

For thousands of years, parents and teachers have used memorable stories called fables to teach simple moral lessons to children.

In the Dino Tales by AV² series, a group of dinosaur friends experience adventure and opportunities to learn important values.

In *Show and Tell,* Grandpa Jake teaches Troy and Chantal that it is best to ask permission before taking something that belongs to someone else. They learn that being unkind to others hurts everyone involved.

This AV² media enhanced book comes alive with...

Animated Video
Watch a custom animated movie.

Try This!
Complete activities and hands-on experiments.

Key Words
Study vocabulary, and complete a matching word activity.

Quiz
Test your knowledge.

Why should you be kind to others?

AV² Storytime Navigation

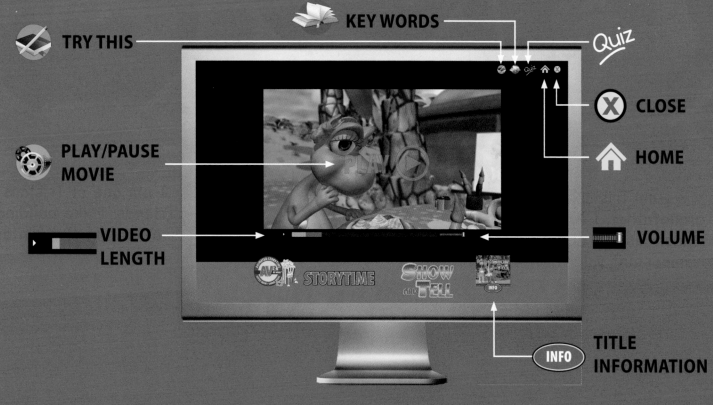

KEY WORDS

TRY THIS

Quiz

X CLOSE

PLAY/PAUSE MOVIE

HOME

VIDEO LENGTH

VOLUME

INFO — **TITLE INFORMATION**

3

The Characters

Grandpa Jake
I am Tristan's grandfather. I like to teach lessons about important values.

Chantal
I am one of Tristan's friends. I love camping in the backyard.

Troy
I am one of Tristan's friends. I like building snowmen in the winter.

Tristan
I am Grandpa Jake's grandson. I like hearing fun stories about dinosaurs.

Suds
I am very good at carving soap into animal shapes. I also like to practice good manners.

Dixie
I like planting flowers in my garden. I also like to paint bright, colorful pictures.

Dixie's Mother
I encourage Dixie to tell the truth.

5

The Story

"This pop-up tent is so nice, Grandpa Jake! It's going to be so much fun camping with my friends!" exclaimed Tristan.

"It sure is!" added Chantal, as she joined Tristan and Troy. "I have my sleeping bag and camping gear too!"

A little later, something in Chantal's backpack caught Troy's eye.

Wow! Chantal's flashlight! It's so much cooler than mine. I bet the light is very bright!

14

Dixie loved to paint bright, colorful pictures of flowers and butterflies. She painted on paper, on big leaves, and even on tree bark.

Mr. Nuggin had asked his students to bring to class something they had made. Dixie brought some of her favorite paintings, and Suds brought carved soap bars shaped like animals.

When it was time to go home, Dixie looked over and saw one of Suds's soaps in the shape of a duck.

I have an idea! I could paint it for my mother. It would be so pretty!
And so, Dixie took the soap bar.

Later that day, while Dixie was painting the bar of soap, someone came up behind her.

18

"Hey! That's my soap bar! You're messing it all up!" exclaimed Suds.

"I'm not messing it up. I'm decorating it," said Dixie as she took the soap and ran away.

Suds was very upset. "She took my bar of soap, so I'm going to take her shells!"

When Suds got home, her first thought was, I'd better hide these shells! She put the shells on her bed. Just then she heard her mother calling, so she sat on the shells to hide them. Crunch!

"Oh no!" cried Suds as she jumped up. "I crushed the shells when I sat on them! Dixie will be so angry at me!"

When Mother came in the room and saw the broken shells and the tears in Suds's eyes, she knew something was wrong. Suds told her mother about what had happened.

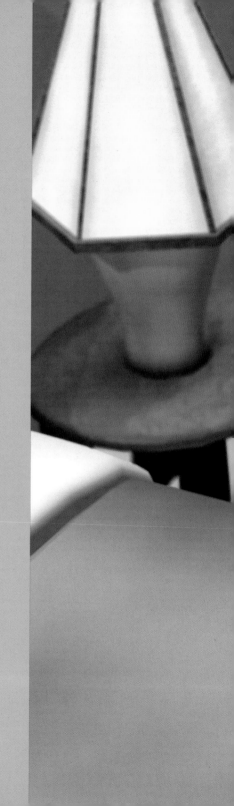

21

"Dixie will probably be sad, but it's better that you tell her the truth," said Dixie's mother. "You were upset that Dixie took your soap, but you shouldn't have taken her shells. When you do something unkind to others, even if you think you have a good reason, it hurts them, and it hurts you too."

"You're right, Mom. I'll tell Dixie about her shells and apologize."

23

The next day at Dixie's house, Suds said, "I took your shells because I was angry at you for taking my soap. I accidentally broke some of them. I'm so sorry!"

Dixie was sad, but then she said, "Actually, I'm the one who should be saying sorry. I should have asked before taking your soap."

"I forgive you!" Suds replied. "You can keep the soap."

"I have an idea for something we can do with these broken shells," Dixie said. "We can glue them to the outside of a box to decorate it. It can be our friendship box."

"I forgive you. And I'm sorry for getting mad at you," said Chantal.

"I'm sorry for wasting your batteries, Chantal. You can use my batteries if you like," said Troy.

"That's much better," said Grandpa Jake. "And you know, I might have a new set of batteries that you can have, Chantal."

"Thank you for helping us work this out, Grandpa Jake! And thank you for the story!"

29

Moral
of the Story

The things we do affect others. If we treat our friends the way we would like to be treated ourselves, we will make them very happy. And in the end, we will be very happy too!

SHOW AND TELL Quiz

1 What did Troy find in Chantal's backpack?

2 What did Dixie love to paint?

3 What did Dixie do with Suds's bar of soap?

4 How did Suds break Dixie's shells?

5 How did Dixie and Suds use the broken shells?

6 Why did Troy tell Chantal he was sorry?

Answers:
1. Her flashlight
2. Pictures of flowers and butterflies
3. Paint it for her mother
4. She sat on them.
5. To decorate their friendship box
6. He wasted the batteries in her flashlight.

Check out www.av2books.com for your animated storytime media enhanced book!

1. Go to www.av2books.com

2. Enter book code   K 2 7 4 2 3 2

3. Fuel your imagination online!

www.av2books.com

AV² Storytime Navigation

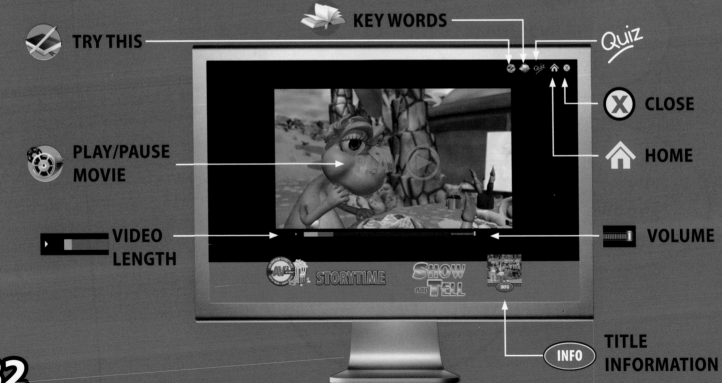

KEY WORDS

TRY THIS

Quiz

CLOSE

PLAY/PAUSE MOVIE

HOME

VIDEO LENGTH

VOLUME

TITLE INFORMATION

INFO